Topic: My Country in the World   **Subtopic:** Sports of the World

Notes to Parents and Teachers:

As a child becomes more familiar reading books, it is importa[nt] ... to rely on and use reading strategies more independently to ... figure out words they don't know.

REMEMBER: PRAISE IS A GREAT MOTIVATOR!

Here are some praise points for beginning readers:

• I saw you get your mouth ready to say the first letter of that word.
• I like the way you used the picture to help you figure out that word.
• I noticed that you saw some sight words you knew how to read!

Book Ends for the Reader!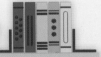

Here are some reminders before reading the text:

• Point to each word you read to make it match what you say.

• Use the picture for help.

• Look at and say the first letter sound of the word.

• Look for sight words that you know how to read in the story.

• Think about the story to see what word might make sense.

Words to Know Before You Read

basketball

cricket

flag

Olympics

soccer

stars

stripes

taekwondo

My Favorite SPORT

By
Robert Rosen
Illustrated by
Nina de Polonia

Rourke
Educational Media
rourkeeducationalmedia.com

Oscar and Olivia watch the TV.

They watch the Olympics.

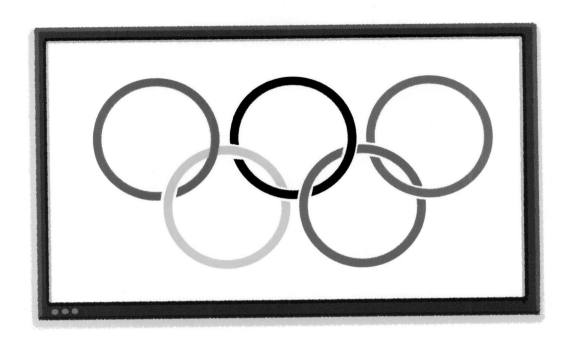

Look at that flag.

I have never seen it before.

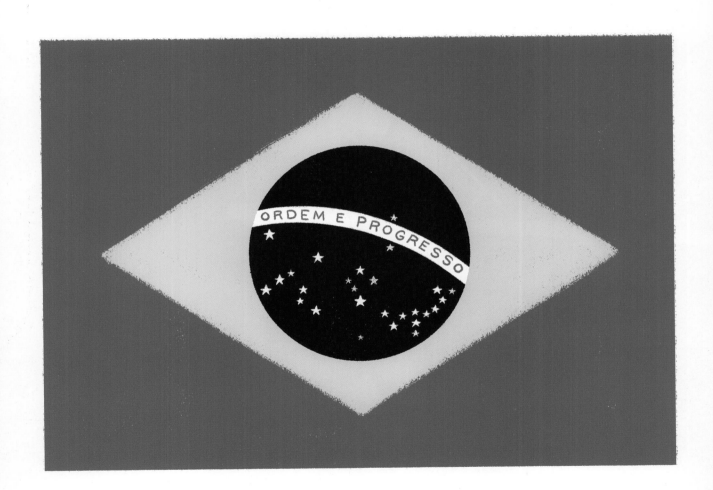

It is Brazil's flag.

Look at that flag.

It is white and red.

That is England's flag.

They are good at cricket.

Look at that flag.

It has stars and stripes.

That is America's flag.

They are good at basketball.

I know that flag.

That is South Korea.

They are good at taekwondo.

I'm good at taekwondo, too.

21

Book Ends for the Reader

I know...

1. What did Oscar and Olivia watch?

2. Which flag had Oscar never seen?

3. What country is good at taekwondo?

I think ...

1. Have you ever watched the Olympics?

2. What is your favorite sport?

3. Is there a sport that you haven't tried?

Book Ends for the Reader

What happened in this book?

Look at each picture and talk about what happened in the story.

About the Author

Robert Rosen lives in South Korea with his wife, son and dog. He has taught kindergarten and elementary students since 2010. He likes to travel the world riding new roller coasters.

About the Illustrator

Nina de Polonia was born in the Philippines in 1985. She has loved drawing ever since she could hold a pencil. Aside from illustrating children's books, she's also a crocheter, calligrapher, herb gardener, and a full-time mom.

Library of Congress PCN Data

My Favorite Sport / Robert Rosen

ISBN (hard cover) 978-1-68342-716-2
ISBN (soft cover) 978-1-68342-768-1
ISBN (e-Book) 978-1-68342-820-6
Library of Congress Control Number: 2017935432

Rourke Educational Media
Printed in the United States of America, North Mankato, Minnesota

© 2018 Rourke Educational Media

www.rourkeeducationalmedia.com

Edited by: Debra Ankiel
Art direction and layout by: Rhea Magaro-Wallace
Cover and interior Illustrations by: Nina de Polonia